This book belongs to
my friend:

_____

A NOTE TO PARENTS

Oswald enjoys having many wonderful friends. But in *A Little Nap*, he finds that friendship sometimes requires putting others' needs ahead of his own desires. Even though he is tired, Oswald does not hesitate to help his friends, and in the end, he is justly rewarded.

Ask your child about Oswald's behavior as his attempts to nap are continually thwarted. How does Oswald treat his friends? Does he become cranky or annoyed? Does he help them as best he can? Based on his attitude and actions, how does Oswald feel about his friends? Ask your child what he would do in a similar situation.

Help your child cultivate long-lasting friendships. Teach him to be sensitive, kind, and generous. Explain that friendship is a two-way street: stress that he should treat his friends the same way he wants them to treat him. Be sure to model this behavior. If your child sees you and your friends display thoughtfulness, patience, and respect toward one another, he will quickly learn the essential ingredients of a healthy, enduring friendship.

Learning Fundamental: **social skills**

For more parent and kid-friendly activities, go to www.nickjr.com.

A LITTLE NAP

Published by Scholastic Inc., 90 Old Sherman Turnpike, Danbury, CT 06816
SCHOLASTIC and associated logos are trademarks and/or registered trademarks of Scholastic Inc.

ISBN 0-7172-6637-0

Printed in the U.S.A.

First Scholastic Printing, June 2003

A LITTLE NAP

by
Dan Yaccarino

illustrated by
Antoine Guilbaud

SCHOLASTIC INC.

New York   Toronto   London   Auckland   Sydney
Mexico City   New Delhi   Hong Kong   Buenos Aires

Oswald the octopus and his pet hot dog, Weenie,
were painting the backyard fence.

"Gosh, Weenie, this sure is hard work!" said Oswald.
"But we're almost finished!"
"Bark! Bark!" said Weenie.

Oswald yawned. So did Weenie.

"I'm sleepy," Oswald said. "Maybe we can finish painting the fence later."

They both decided that a nap was a pretty good idea,
so they went inside.

Oswald and Weenie got quite comfortable and were all set to take a little nap.

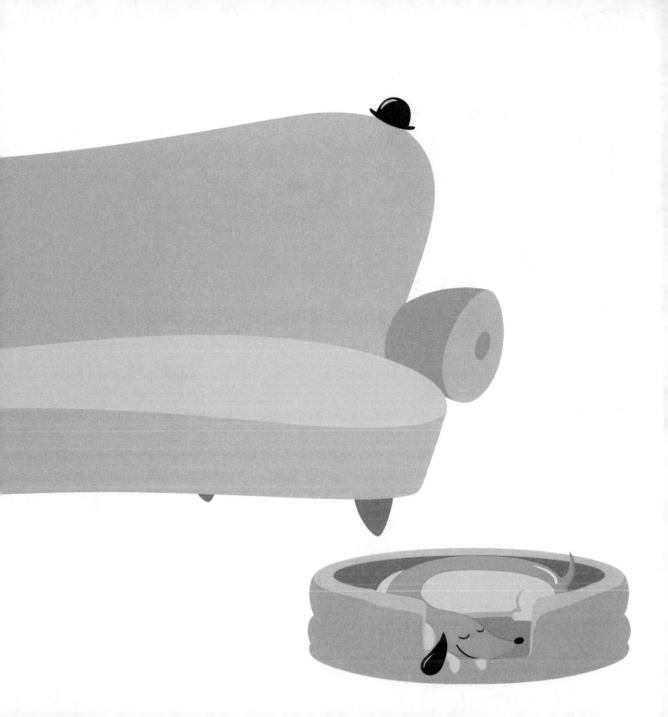

Knock, knock, knock.
"Someone is at the door," Oswald said. He opened it.

"Hey, Oswald!" shouted Daisy. "My bicycle is making a funny noise. Can you please help me fix it?"

"Allow me," Oswald said, tightening the bolts on Daisy's bicycle.

"Thanks mucho!" exclaimed Daisy.

"You're quite welcome!" said Oswald.

Now for a little nap.

Knock, knock, knock.
"Someone is at the door," Oswald said. He opened it.

"Oh, hello, Oswald!" said Madame Butterfly.
"Boo, boo, boo!" said Catrina Caterpillar.
"Catrina's rattle isn't making any noise," Madame Butterfly explained. "Can you please help us fix it?"

"Allow me," Oswald said. He unscrewed the rattle and put in some beans to make it jingle.

"Thank you ever so," said Madame Butterfly.

"Gooby, gooby," said Catrina Caterpillar.

"You're quite welcome!" said Oswald.

Now for a little nap.

Knock, knock, knock.

"Someone is at the door," Oswald said. He opened it.

"Hello, old chum," said Henry. "I'm having trouble opening a very stubborn can of sardines. Can you please help me open it?"

"Allow me," Oswald said, prying open the can
of sardines.

"Much obliged, pal," said Henry.

"You're quite welcome!" said Oswald.

Now for a little nap.

Knock, knock, knock.

"Someone is at the door," Oswald said. He opened it.

"*Greetingth,*" mumbled Egbert, one of the Egg Twins.

"*Yeth! Yeth!*" mumbled Egbert's brother Leo.
"*Greetingth!*"

Oswald laughed. "I see you were both blowing bubbles at the same time!"

"Allow me," Oswald said, gently pulling the Egg Twins apart.

"Most kind of you," mumbled Egbert.
"Yes! Yes! Thanks, dear boy!" mumbled Leo.
"You're quite welcome!" said Oswald.

"It's getting late," Oswald said to Weenie.

"I don't think we're going to be able to take a little nap today, girl," Oswald said. "Let's finish painting the fence."

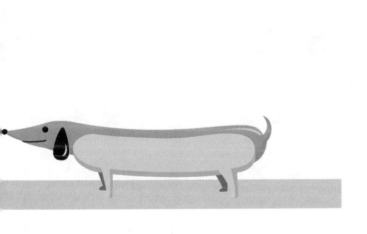

Oswald and Weenie returned to the backyard.
They couldn't believe their eyes! The fence was
completely painted!

"Surprise!" everyone shouted.

"Since you helped us," Daisy explained, "we wanted to do something nice for you, too."

"Thank you," Oswald said. "I couldn't ask for better friends."

"Bark! Bark!" agreed Weenie.

Now for a little fun.